STERLING CHILDREN'S BOOKS
New York

An Imprint of Sterling Publishing
387 Park Avenue South
New York, NY 10016

Library of Congress Cataloging-in-Publication Data Available

Lot#:
10 9 8 7 6 5 4 3 2 1
03/12

Distributed in Canada by Sterling Publishing
c/o Canadian Manda Group, 165 Dufferin Street
Toronto, Ontario, Canada M6K 3H6
Distributed in the United Kingdom by GMC Distribution Services
Castle Place, 166 High Street, Lewes, East Sussex, England BN7 1XU
Distributed in Australia by Capricorn Link (Australia) Ptd. Ltd.
P.O. Box 704, Sindsor, NSW 2756, Australia

Sterling ISBN 978-1-4027-7229-0

For information about custom editions, special sales, premium and corporate purchases, please contact Sterling Special Sales Department at 800-805-5489 or specialsales@sterlingpublishing.com
www.sterlingpublishing.com/kids

Little Bear's
Baby Brother

By Mary Packard
Illustrated by Lisa McCue

STERLING CHILDREN'S BOOKS
New York

Five little bear cubs yawned and stretched. They were just waking up from a long winter sleep. They heard the *drip, drip, drip* of melting icicles. They heard noisy birds building nests. They heard Mama whisper to Papa Bear, "It's time to get the crib down from the attic. Soon there will be a new baby sleeping in our den."

"Yippee!" the cubs squealed at once.

"When will our new baby be born?" Little Bear asked.

"When all the snow has melted and the ground is soft and green," Mama replied.

"That long?" she complained.

"Our baby will be here before you know it," said Mama. "Until then, we will be very, very busy. Everyone will need to help get ready."

They painted the crib.

They hung up new curtains.

They even made a sign that said WELCOME.

No one was busier than Little Bear. Each day she scoured the forest for the prettiest things she could find.

One morning Papa Bear helped her make a mobile with all of her treasures. She hoped the new baby would like her present. Little Bear placed the mobile on a rock and left it outside to dry.

After a while, Mole scurried by. He spied the mobile at once.
"Who would throw away something so fine?" he cried. "A door
knocker like this will surely come in handy!"

So Mole took the *doorknocker* and hurried off to his home.

"Now I will hear whenever someone comes to visit," he said happily.

Mole set out to find string to hang his new doorknocker.
Soon after, Raccoon happened by. "What luck!" he said.
"With this fishing lure I can catch many fish at one time!"
Raccoon took the *fishing lure* and placed it on the grass by
the side of the pond. Then off he went to fetch his fishing pole.

Just then Owl swooped down, "Such a nice wind chime should not be left on the ground," he declared. He picked up the *wind chime* and carried it off to hang in a tree right outside his home.

That afternoon the cubs heard their Papa call to them.

"The baby is here," he shouted happily.

The cubs followed Papa into the house. Little Bear marveled at the baby's size. The baby's little paws were just like her own, only so much tinier.

One by one, the cubs brought special presents to their baby brother. Little Bear went to get her mobile.

She ran outside, but the mobile was not where she had left it.

She searched in the bushes. She looked in the tall grasses
and inside hollow logs near her den. Finally, she gave up and
went inside.

"I'm sorry I don't have a present for you, Baby," she said.

Just then a gust of wind swept through the trees, spreading musical sounds all through the room.

What could be making those beautiful sounds? they all wondered.

The cubs rushed outside. *Whoosh!* The wind rustled the trees, and there it was again—tinkling sounds from above. Little Bear looked up and what did she see? There was her mobile, swaying in the breeze!

How did my mobile get way up there? she wondered.

Little Bear scurried up the tree and down again in a flash, clutching her mobile safely in her paws.

Papa Bear attached the beautiful mobile to the crib. Then Little Bear gave it a spin. The baby followed the sparkly objects with his eyes. He kicked his tiny paws at the pretty sounds.

"I knew you would like this mobile," Little Bear said.
"I made it just for you." Then she was quiet for a moment.
"I just wonder how it got way up in that tree!"